FULL ARMOR MAGAZINE

FALL 2010 ISSUE

Dragondreamz Publications

Full Armor Magazine
Fall 2010 issue

Dragondreamz Publications

ISBN: 978-0-9828116-1-0

Editor: K. Crumley

Full Armor Magazine
Fall 2010

In this issue:

From the Editor's Quill

…the issue that almost wasn't.

Wow. This has been a hard issue to pull together. Believe it or not, this was harder than our debut issue, which premiered in July 2010.

There were several contributing factors to this. The first, obviously, content issues. I was flooded with manuscripts...but so few of them actually fit what *Full Armor Magazine* is actually about. I was faced with the challenge of keeping true to the integrity and core message of Full Armor. I had to reject more stories and poems this time, than I did the first time around. It began to make me feel bad (knowing full well what rejection feels like). But, I had to hold true our mission statement and core message. I also realized I need a "keep it clean" message to add to our submissions. A lot of stories contained foul language. While I do not regard myself as a prude by any means; and I do acknowledge that sometimes in storytelling it is necessary to keep your stories believable. But, certain words and expressions can offend our readership.

The biggest issue however was my heath, as I have been dealing with endometriosis and some digestive issues which had turned out to be colitis. There have been days when I haven't felt like working…or was too sick to even sit up at the computer.

Also, my "day job" had its usual adverse affect. Shortage of staff, and employees taking vacations meant me putting in a lot of overtime.

Then I remembered that God said he'll provide what I need…whatever I need…to keep this magazine going, for as long as he wants me to. And today, Sunday, September 05, 2010 I received a big spiritual push in the right direction.

I want to thank my wonderful, patient, and talented contributors: Jay Faulkner (you are in my prayers), Gigi Austin, Leila Fortier, and William B. Hurst.

I would also like to thank my friends and fellow indie authors, Jon Fitch V for letting me review his novel *One Hero a Savior,* and Marlayne Giron author of *The Victor* for letting me interview her regarding her book and its interactive lesson plan.

May you find something to enjoy and be entertained by in this issue.

~K. Crumley
Editor
Full Armor Magazine

Many thanks to our patient, and understanding contributors. John Finch V and Marlayne Giron, thanks for letting me feature your awesome books!

Thanks to my sister Tracy A. McCann, who years ago provided the illustrations for *The Golden Rose,* and my niece Mia Nicole who inspired me to revive and re-edit my children's stories.

Thanks to dreamstime.com, one resource I cannot live without!

Thanks mostly to God, for being especially provident this season.

Book Review

John Fitch V's *One Hero, A Savior*

K. Crumley

Imagine Tolkien waking up in his own Middle Earth…
CS Lewis stepping through his wardrobe, into a real, live Narnia…
L. Frank Baum being swept up in a cyclone, landing in Oz…
The Creator winds up in a land of his own creation.
That's the premise for John Fitch V's. Christian Fantasy *One Hero, A Savior*.

In the midst of a storm, young Red Sox fan Preston is on his way to meet his sweetheart Lynnabeth. Then, tragedy strikes as Preston is hit by a sports car.

He wakes up in a beautiful land, where the sun is shinning brightly and realizes he's not in Boston anymore. Soon he discovers that he is in a land of his own creation, Arida, The domain of the fantasy stories he writes. Arida is populated by innocent Halflings, noble Elves, wicked Dwarves and malicious Orcs.

Preston is faced with many trials, and challenges…and must accept his destiny as Lord over Arida.

The story is full of clever Christian symbolism, even right down to the naming of Preston's arch enemy. The imagery and descriptions make Arida appear right before your minds eye. And, Preston is the most instantly likeable fantasy character since Harry Potter.

I highly recommend *One Hero, A Savior* to fantasy fans of all ages.

Four our struggle
Is not against flesh and blood,
But against the rulers,
Against the authorities,
Against the powers of this dark world
And against the spiritual forces of evil
In the heavenly realms.

Ephisians 6:12

Thanks Given

Gigi Austin

Thanks given,
we turn toward joy
full of bell
sounds of traditionally
new intentions ringing
hopeful
this year
that maybe those 10 pounds
will disappear
before
Easter Sunday
resurrects old habits
cross by nature
grave in their ways
memorial days we remember them
and those who've fought
in dependence
a fourth of what we have we need
and we are back to grateful
for the surplus
that passeth all understanding
blessing us rich and
happy
holy days
I wish to you
until the leaves
turn
fall
again.

~Drink~

Leila Fortier

Did

You notice

How your lips

Fit perfectly

In the

Palm

Of

My

Hand?

These hands

Are the cup of life

That you were meant

To drink from~ My love

The vineyard~ Your mind

The press~ Come drink

The wine of your

…Harvest…

~You~
Leila Fortier

*

You
Made the sound
Of one hand clapping...And I fell
To your feet in prayer...Let this silence fill you
With the hushed voice of me ~ Like a breeze
Upon your heart...and the
Aftertaste of
Wine
*

~Know This~

Leila Fortier

Know this:
That in my vast imperfections…I have loved you perfectly
For I have found a perfect love within me~
Know this:
When I part this earth on my appointed hour…I shall never have left you
For when my body turns to dust…I will ever be a single breath
In form of a living prayer~

1 July 1916

W.B. Hurst

Marie, if bullets come
from my side, remember
to keep my casket
shut with stone.
I will not stay in
a trench,
but crawl to the other side.
My comrades are bound, beyond
the line that I must cross.
Let our children hear
that their father died
for them.

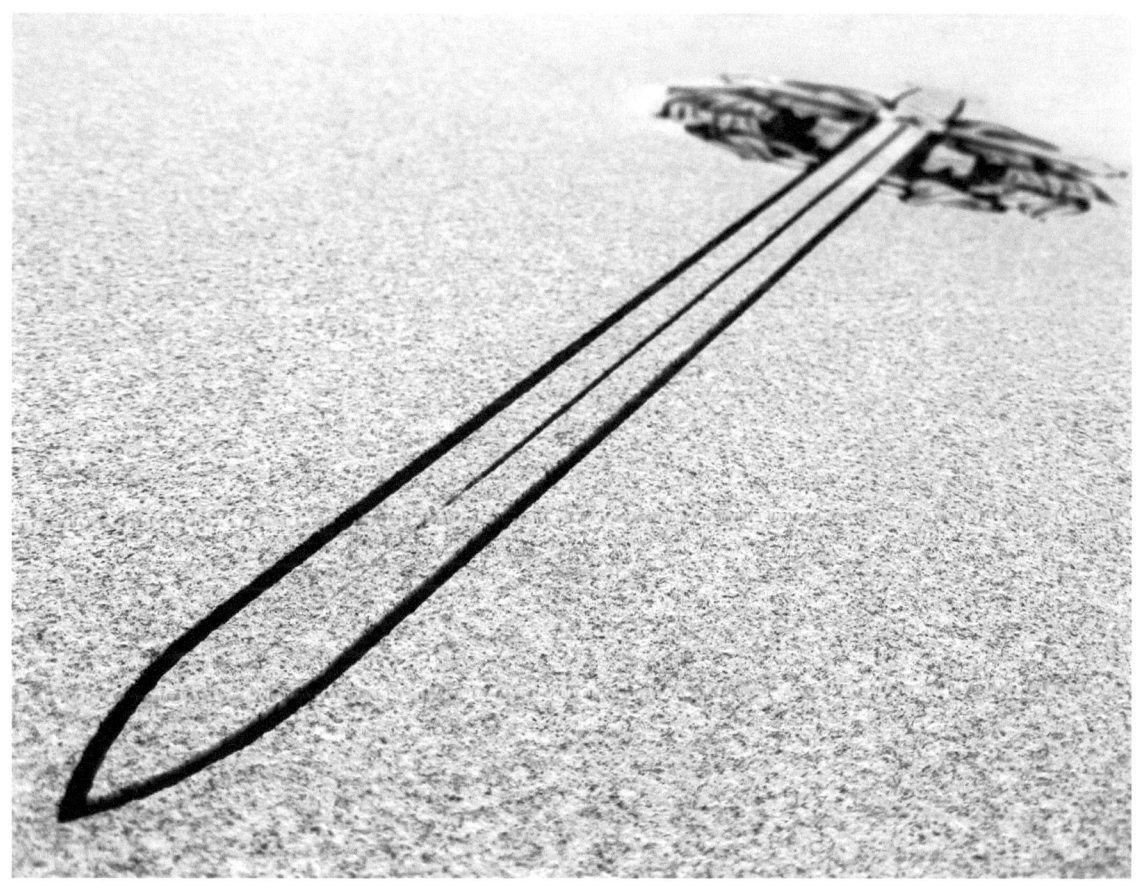

Eyes Wide Open

Jay Faulkner

The morning Sun streamed in through the window like shafts of pure gold. Illuminating the room with an almost too intense light, cascading over everything like waves from a yellow ocean, the sunlight brought hints of burnished orange and golden honey to everything that it touched. Motes of dust floated languidly, like once-bright stars reliving their now faded glory. Light and airy already, with only a large bed, a bedside cabinet and a full-length, wooden-framed mirror to fill its space, the room was an oasis of calm tranquility. The air in the room was still, though not oppressively so.

An edge of expectation hung in the silence; this was a portentous day, one that was just waiting to begin.

"Oh Lord, thank you for this day," Beth Georgia sighed a bittersweet breath of contentment and melancholy, her voice as dry as sandpaper but still full of simple joy.

She was barely perceptible under the covers, the eiderdown hardly swelling as it covered her small frame, and the face that stared out through the windows to the clear Spring day was almost skeletal in it's gauntness. Skin, that could have just as easily been sun-dried leather, was taut against her skull and covered by a network of lines that played out the road map of every one of her years; while not the oldest woman in the World there were days that Beth felt like she was, and today - her one hundredth and second birthday - was definitely one of them.

Deep brown eyes gazed out through the window, their keenness belaying the passage of years that they had watched. If eyes were the windows of the soul then Beth's looked into a self-less life, a worthy life, a long life, lived well. In a body that was beyond frailty, beyond miraculous, the eyes sparkled with a youthfulness that brought a smile to all who looked into them. Just as it brought a smile to the face of Nina Georgia, Beth's only great-granddaughter, as she quietly walked into the room and paused to stare, with obvious love, at the small woman in the bed.

Standing at just barely over five foot three, and small boned, Nina was almost the image of how Beth had looked at her age. Nina, of course, never realised the small pang of fatality that her appearance evoked in her great-grandmother as she had never seen a photo of Beth at that age. For Beth, though, it was like looking into the past and an image of the seventeen-year-old girl she would never be again.

The age difference was never a factor in their relationship, though; Beth and Nina were as close as two people could be. Love that transcended the generations filled them and they knew without knowing that their souls were linked in a way that the rest of the family could never quite match. Beth and her husband George, who had been dead and buried for over forty years, had had seven children. Over the years her family - and no matter how large or widespread it became it would always be HER family - had grown to include eighteen grandchildren, all of whom Beth loved completely.

Then, seventeen years ago to the day, sharing Beth's own birthday, Nina was born. At that moment Beth realised that, though she loved all of her family with her whole heart, she loved Nina more; she loved Nina with her heart and soul.

"You going to stand there all day child?" Beth asked without looking around, her voice rasping but filled with humor.

Nina laughed as she stepped into the room, her arms clasped around the large bouquet of wild flowers that she had spent the morning picking. Beth loved nature but had been bedridden for nearly two years now, watching the World pass by outside her window and experiencing it only through the small parts that Nina regularly brought inside for her.

As she reached the bed Nina struggled to hold the flowers together as she leant over and gently kissed Beth's forehead.

"Happy birthday, Mama," she smiled using the name that the whole family - and most of the people in the small town where she had spent her whole life - called Beth. No matter the actual relationship to people Beth treated everyone like her child; the archetypal mother figure.

"… and a happy birthday to you as well, my darlin' child," Beth's eyes twinkled with mirth. "And am I to take it that the small forest in your arms is for me?"

"No, they were just lying at the door so I thought that I would bring them in and put them in the trash, I mean we don't want them stinking up the neighbourhood!" Nina quipped, her own eyes sparkling.

Moving faster then expected, for someone as frail as she was, Beth's hand snatched a small white rose from Nina's arms. Taking a small step backwards Nina laughed as Beth held the rose to her nose and inhaled, deeply.

"Ah child if only everyone in the neighbourhood could smell the sweetness of the rose the way I do, but if you don't get those poor things in some water they won't be lastin' long at all," Beth said around the flower.

"I'll go get the vase then come back and tell you all about what Johnny is doing for me tonight," Nina said with a smile of excitement, winking at Beth as the rose fell to the pillow beside her head.

Beth allowed herself a small smile as she watched Nina walk through the doorway, and out of sight. 'So young but already settled with that nice Johnny,' she thought to herself, 'but then who am I to worry about that when I knew that my George was the man for me at her age too?' The memory of her husband brought, as it always did, a smile to Beth's face and she turned towards the window again, watching the sunlight illuminate the dust.

'Little stairways to Heaven,' she thought to herself, remembering how her mother had told her – oh so many years ago - how the light that streamed down was sent from God above to allow Angels to come down and help people. In a life filled with pain and hardship that little piece of her mother, whose face she couldn't quite remember anymore, brought Beth comfort.

"Ah but Lord above, Beth Georgia, you think that you'd be too old for such nonsense now, wouldn't you?" she muttered to herself.

"Too old to believe in angels?"

The voice filled Beth's ears with the taste of honey, it filled her eyes with the smell of freshly mown grass and it filled her nose with the colour of warm barley. Her head swam, her senses overwhelmed, and for a second she couldn't catch her breath. For that second it felt like she was drowning, like everything was slowing down, fading, and getting darker.

… And then, suddenly, it was all so very clear again.

The sunlight streaming though the window seemed more vibrant, seemed more alive than before, and the motes of dust now visibly danced around each other. The blue sky outside the window was an azure that she had never seen before and the small white clouds that dotted the clear blue expanse moved past with unbelievable speed.

Remembering the voice she turned her head and a small gasp escaped her mouth as she stared at the figure that stood there, at her side.

'So beautiful,' she thought to herself as she gazed at the man - the youth - who stood gazing at her fondly. An immaculate white suit, obviously tailored to fit his lithe form, gleamed as if with a hidden backlight. The shirt - open at the

collar to reveal golden, sun blanched skin - was a paler shade of white again. Blonde hair fell to his shoulders and piercing blue eyes stared at Beth intently.

"Thank you Beth," the man smiled graciously.

Beth shook her head as if to clear it. 'Damn you woman, you are getting old, talkin' out loud like that when a strange man walks into your bedroom!' she thought to herself. Though she knew that she should she didn't feel afraid, or alarmed; only a quiet calmness, washing over her, tinged with curiosity.

"You know, if you have come here lookin' for money, or anythin' like that, you are out of luck sonny, I don't have anythin' of value here!" Beth said to him calmly, her gaze unwavering.

"I am not here for your money Mam; you are wrong though, you DO have something that is very valuable here," the figure said with small smile as he took a step towards the bed, hands swinging gently by his side. "Priceless even."

He sat down gently beside Beth, reaching out to lay one hand on top of her own and smiled as a look of wonder played over her face. Beth's eyes widened at the stranger's touch. For as long as she could remember, for too many damn years, her body had been betraying her; arthritis had spread through most of her joints and her hands, especially, constantly ached. When the stranger placed his hand over hers, however, the pain left.

Realisation began to set in and Beth's eyes widened even more as a small, almost shy, smile played across her lips.

"You have a beautiful smile Beth," the young man said, smiling in return.

"Oh shush now, boy; you are far too young to be talkin' all sweet like that to me, and I am far too old to be listenin' to your pretty tongue," Beth said, but her smile deepened nonetheless.

"Well I am not as young as you think that I am Beth, so in my eyes you are not old at all," the stranger laughed as he reached up to tenderly stroke Beth's cheek.

A shudder of pleasure ran through her as she felt the memory of every pain, every ache, and every swollen joint and hardened artery, disappear. For the first time in as long as she remembered she felt alive, truly alive. It was glorious. Unbidden, but not even trying to stop them, tears of joy streamed down her cheeks as she stared into the eyes of the beautiful stranger in front of her.

"What was that you said a moment ago ... about being too old to believe?" she whispered.

"I asked if you were too old to believe in angels Beth, but you didn't answer me," he repeated gently as he stared at her. " ... so, do you?"

"What?"

"Believe Beth, believe?"

Beth gave a shudder, a small shiver that her mother would have claimed meant someone had walked over her grave. 'Over one hundred years, who would have thought it?' Beth asked herself quietly. Good years, years filled with love and happiness - enough to outweigh the years of hardship and struggle: the years of racism and fear.

One hundred and two years of life.

Beth smiled to herself as with some effort - but not as much as she was expecting - she raised herself up on the pillows and stared directly into the young man's face; her eyes twinkled as they reflected the pure and simple expression of joy on his expression.

"What do I call you, sonny?" Beth asked, avoiding the question.

"I have many names, Mama, but you can call me Azrael - if you wish?" he replied, gently, holding out a hand expectantly.

At the name Beth gave a small sigh. She had always been a faithful woman, had read her scriptures and remembered them for as long back as she could recall. The name was known to her, as was the duty that he carried out.

"Well, Azrael, I guess that I am not too old after all, am I?" she said with a small smile. "So why don't you just take me home?"

Reaching out she placed her small hand in his own, smiling at the look of shock that played over his face ever so briefly. Gripping the hand that engulfed her own she laughed, fully and vibrantly, her voice sounding strange until she realised that she could hear no trace of frailty or age in it.

"What's that matter Azrael, not what you were expectin'?" she asked teasingly.

"Well I have to admit that I thought that you might have questions, might have concerns, might even argue ..."

"I have spent one hundred and two years trusting in the Lord boy, and I am not goin' to stop doin' that now just because He has decided that it is time to call me home. I am ready; I've had a good life and now I'm prepared to meet my Maker" she interrupted.

"So you are ready to leave the World, and your family, behind?" he asked tenderly.

"Ready? No I wouldn't say that I am ready, but I knew that this day would come and I am not afraid to take the journey; I am not afraid to leave. I accepted a long time ago that this day would come, and now it's here," she said with quiet dignity.

"You are an amazing woman, Beth Georgia, and know that your family will be well and will always love and remember you," Azrael nodded and smiled at her warmly.

"So is it time?" Beth asked quietly, a tremor in her voice. "... is it time for me to die?"

Azrael laughed, holding out his hands and clasping her own in his. Pulling her to her feet he turned her to face the mirror and she gasped in shock. The reflection was not the frail shell of a woman that she had been for the last few decades; the girl that she remembered being, the girl that she was inside - that she had always been – stared back. She was young again. She was herself again.

"No Beth, it is not time for you to die, my child," Azrael said gently as he stepped in close and embraced her in his strong arms. "That happened before we even started talking.

Over his shoulder Beth saw herself - the old woman that she had been – still lying in the bed, unmoving. She placed her head against his chest as she realised that her life - her pain - was really over and that the conversation with the angel of death had simply been to ease her on her journey. As his arms closed tightly around her she gasped in surprise as she felt the feather-light tickle on her face.

Wrapping his wings around her, Azrael became ensconced in a nimbus of golden light and, when she was safely cocooned within, he looked out through the window, his gaze traveling along the pathway of light.

"Father, we are ready," he said gently, and then smiled as the light intensified around him.

Nina gasped, both hands going up involuntarily to her mouth. The vase fell to the floor and shattered with a crash as glass and water exploded around the room. Flowers scattered all over and lay, unnoticed, as tears filled her eyes.

She watched the woman who had shaped her entire life lay unmoving on the bed, her chest still and quiet. She took a step forwards and reached out to lay a hand, gently, on the still-warm skin of the old woman. A small, sad, smile played over her face as Nina leaned down and kissed Beth's forehead - not noticing the small feather that floated gently to the floor near the mirror.

Wiping the tears from her cheeks she stepped out of the room, looking back as she burned the beatific expression on her great grandmother's face into her memory for all time.

With her face to the sky, and an expression of complete and utter peace on her face, Beth Georgia lay still and unmoving, staring into the Heavens with eyes wide open.

Do not fret because of evil men
Or be envious of those who do wrong.
For, like the grass they will soon wither;
Like green plants they will soon die away.

Trust in the Lord and do good;
Dwell in the land and enjoy safe pasture.
Delight yourself in the Lord,
And he will give you the desires
Of your heart.

Psalm 37: 1-4

To the Author of *The Victor* Goes the Spoils!
An interview with Marlayne Giron

Image courtesty of Marlaye Giron.

Recently, I've become friends with Marlayne Giron, Author of the Christian Epic Fantasy *The Victor.* This is not your typical young adult fantasy book…it also has an accompanying lesson plan for students.

While many independently published authors are knocking on doors trying to get their books the attention that they deserve, Marlayne is breaking through barriers…Reaching not only school districts and festivals, but a few famous names and faces such as Sarah Palin, Amy Grant, and Author Nicholas Sparks.

Next stop Hollywood?

I asked Marlayne a few questions about her wonderful book, and what plans are in store for her and *The Victor.*

Q. What has been your greatest source of inspiration in the writing of this novel?

Marlayne: The primary inspiration came 30 years ago while listening to the song Fairytale by Amy Grant on her Father's Eyes albums. The verse in the song which gave me the lightbulb was: *two princes wage the battle for eternity but the victor has been known from the start.* It created a picture of Satan in black armor and Jesus in shining armor crossing swords over the bride of Christ. The rest of my influence are the movies and books I love to watch/read. Old classic swashbuckler, King Arthur and the Knights of the Round Table, Three Musketeers, First Knight, Excaliber and of course I have been greatly influenced by the books I love (Lord of the Rings) and anything by Stephen R. Lawhead.

Q. Recently, you got to meet Amy Grant...share a little bit of that experience with us.

Marlayne: I expected to be really nervous but it was a very surreal moment. I only had about 90 seconds with her. She is very tall and beautiful. I showed her the book, told her that it was inspired by her song 30 years ago. I also mentioned that I used to work for John Styll (now President of the Gospel Music Association) 30 years ago and that I also had a daughter named Karina. I was told not to touch her first so I let her put her arm around me for the photo. It was clear from her comments that she has not yet read the book though she has had it for over a year. If I had stayed a few hours longer I could have spent some actual time with her on board her bus but it was a last minute decision on her part.

Q. You also have a very challenging and engaging student lesson plan to accompany *The Victor*. Did you create the lesson plan all on your own, or did you have help from teachers or others in the education field?

Marlayne: One of the oldest friends of my husband, Michael, is a public middle school teacher. I approached her about creating a lesson plan and she spent half a day with me showing me the elements that should go into it. I also had The Victor Lexile scored and the minimum reading level is middle school (both genders). The Lesson Plan was created for those who home school junior high and high school students. It is available in hard copy format only on my website (using Paypal) but there is a free downloadable student workbook in Word for Windows format that just has the questions on my website at: http://thevictor.tatepublishing.net/?page_id=890

Q. I'm aware that you're in contact with people to try to sell movie rights for *The Victor*. And, I wish you great luck with that. Do you envision any well-known actors playing these characters?

Marlayne: The only well known actors I think I would like to cast would be for Eloth (Sean Connery - who may be too old now) and for Penloth (Gerard Butler). Everyone else I think I would like for them to be unknown actors (just the way Star Wars was).

Q. How old were you when you started writing?

Marlayne: I wrote stories as a kid for school assignments but really got into it when I was 12 when my best friend at the time, Lisa, showed me a story she had written for us at one of our many sleepovers. She had put us in as characters into our favorite television show at the time (*The Six Million Dollar Man* in the early 1970s). It was so much fun that I wrote the next one and together we wrote hundreds of short stories. Then, Lisa, who wanted to be a school teacher, began red-marking and almost grading my English grammar, spelling and punctuation. It so infuriated me that I became determined to write a story she couldn't find fault with. So I guess you could say that I owe a lot of my writing ability to all the stories we wrote as kids as well as all the books I've read because I never went to college or studied writing.

Q. Are you going to work on another novel?

Marlayne: I am currently working on expanding The Victor for a traditional publisher and I'm also working on a prequel called Sword Brothers featuring two of the more interesting characters from The Victor.

Q. What's the best piece of advice you can give to aspiring writers?

Marlayne: Read a lot, belong to a critique group and never give up on your dream.

Q. Is there anything else you'd like us to know?

Marlayne: I answer every email I get so please feel free to write me at: thevictorbook@sbcglobal.net.

Thank you so much Marlayne, for the interview!

To find out more about Marlayne Giron and *The Victor*, please visit http://www.thevictorbook.com

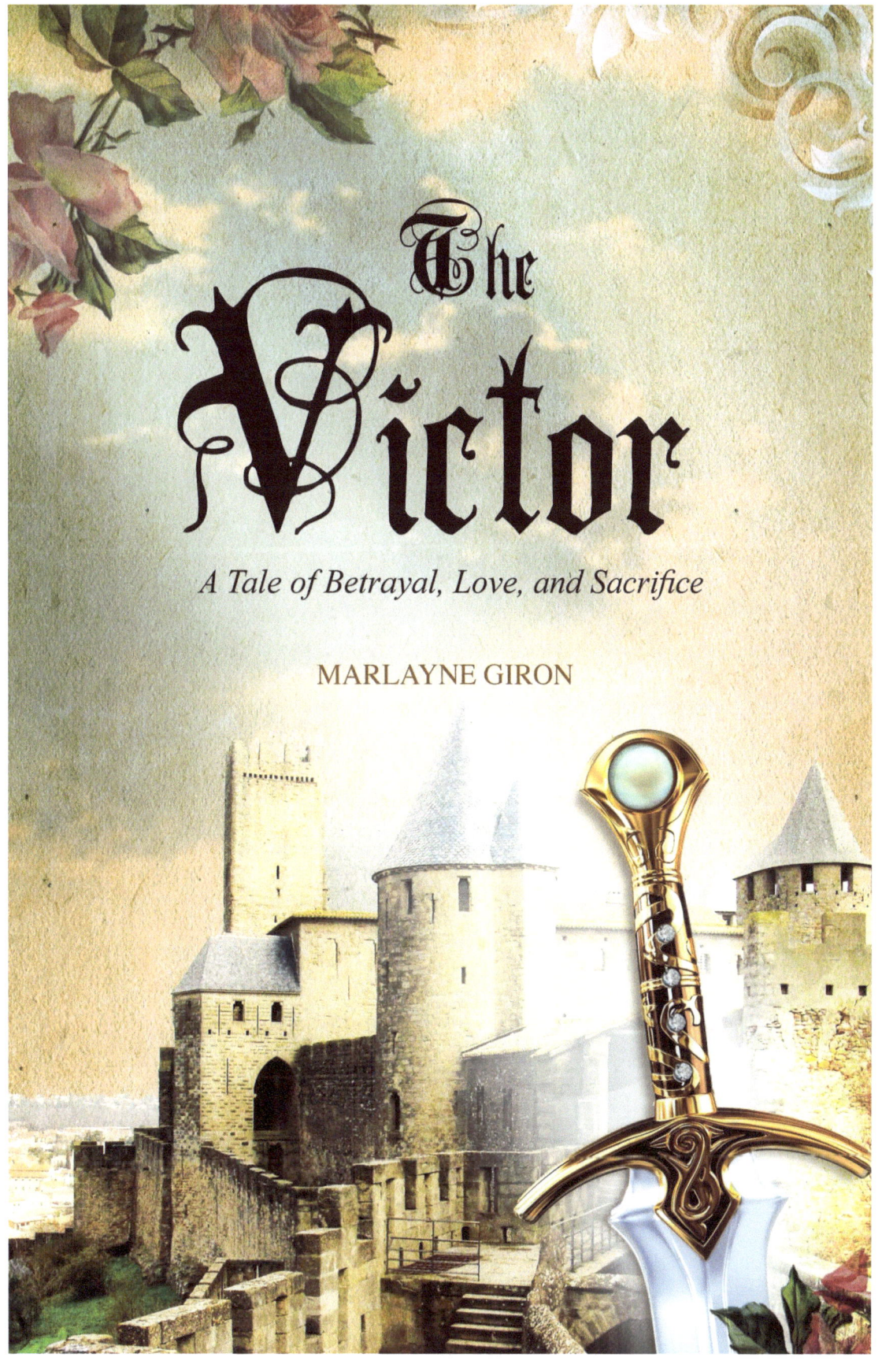

The Victor

A Tale of Betrayal, Love, and Sacrifice

MARLAYNE GIRON

Christian Symbolism Word Search:

    Through the ages people have used Fantasy stories to teach christian principles, and to pass on wise tales from generation to generation.

Fantasy creatures such as unicorns were meant to symbolize Christ, purity, or even virginity. In this puzzle, you will find many words that represent Christianity, Godliness, Purity, and innocence throughout the vast ream of fantasy literature.

```
R I N G S A R M O R E G A
J E H C A S T L E K I N G
O T O L E M A C H W K S R
U D B K S A N P S N N P D
R R B S N I N E I O R E N
N A I D R A U G G I P A N
E Z T P O P H A E N I R P
Y I S L C T R S O L H S M
S W S U I D T I Y S S O O
F W W I N V T T N I D O D
S E O I U A E Z I C N T S
I R L R V I M T H L E H I
I E L L D R O O A L I S W
D R A G O N R I D E R A S
S S H E A W C A L E F Y T
R E Y C G O S D S E E E S
E U L M W D M H J V A R D
L O H P B A E V I C C E F
V I T T I O I L H P S A L
E Y A D R C L I W S O W A
S T E R T A N S H O A E T
Q N D O G G G I S R N R T
U R R E S Y E N R O I K R
E Y R O D L L I I P R O U
S S O O D S O O P K E C S
T W S H P R O P H E T S T
```

WORD LIST:

Unicorns	journey	knowledge
Hobbits	castle	Knight
Cross	principles	King Arthur
Sword	teachings	Camelot
Shield	symbols	Holy Grail
Elves	Deathly Hallows	Dragons
Angels	Rings	Dragonrider
Wizard	Defeat Evil	Sooth Sayer
Prophet	Victory	Spear
Priest	King	armor
Prince	Wisdom	salvation
Warrior	villagers	volcano
friendship	freedom	diety
fellowship	princess	Sun
trust	shield maiden	
quest	guardian	

ANSWERS ON PAGE 41

The Golden Rose

K. Crumley

Illustrations by Tracy A. McCann

Once there lived a beautiful girl named Nicola. She was not wealthy by any means; but her loveliness and caring nature had won her the heart of Grande Duke's son, Xavier to whom she was betrothed. She loved him very much and had thought that they would always be happy together.

However, when their wedding day had arrived young Xavier did not show up at the Chapel. Instead he sent a Paige to relay the message to Nicola, telling her that he cannot marry her. For is family would disown him if he married a peasant; and he would thus lose his wealth and influence.

Nicola's eyes filled up with tears at the sound of the Paige's words. Her heart raced as her face felt flushed. Devastated, she murmured the words "Now my only chance for happiness is gone."

"No child," a kind voice said, "Don't despair. Hold onto your faith. And you'll be happy again soon enough." It was the kindhearted Minister, who was supposed to perform the ceremony. Nicola always thought quite highly of him, "That's easier said than…"

He shushed her, then handed her something. "Take this." It was a small, red velvet satchel. "Plant these seeds in the deepest part of the forest. Then, every time you feel sorrow, shed your tears upon that spot. When the roses bloom you'll find happiness again."

The Minister's words seemed uplifting, but Nicola found it hard to fight her doubts. She took into consideration that devoting her time to planting the seeds would take her mind off of her current grief, "Yes." She said, "That must be what he meant."

She did as he said, and with the tiny sack of seeds in her hand she immediately headed into the forest.

When she arrived at the deepest part of the forest, Nicola opened the small red pouch. In it were two seeds, both shaped like tiny hearts. One was made of pure gold, and the other was sterling silver. She gave them a wary look, and then a snicker. "How can a plant grow from gold? Or silver?" She murmured. She decided to take a chance, and plant the gold one first…and then, she'd see what happens. "Miracles can happen, every day." She said, fighting against doubt and sorrow looming in her mind. "And, I'll never find out…if I don't try."

Nicola planted the seed in the dirt, and then covered it with soil. She sat and prayed that the seed would in fact grow into a beautiful rosebush. She also prayed that her sorrow over losing Xavier would end. She felt her heart break, as she thought of him. She began to cry…

As she wept, tears fell upon the spot where she planted the golden seed. Suddenly, an Angel of Heaven flew down and kissed the ground where her tears fell. A few moments later, a red rosebush sprouted up from the ground. In the center of the rosebush was a golden heart-shaped bud that had not yet bloomed.

"Thank you," Nicola said, "This is the most beautiful rosebush I have ever seen."

The Angel smiled, kissed Nicola's brow and then flew back to Heaven.

Nicola went home that night, amazed at what she had seen.

The next day, Nicola returned to the center of the forest. Still feeling heartbroken over the love that she'd lost, she shed tears upon the rosebush. Her tears caused the roses to bloom. They were all bright crimson red, except for the rose in the center. It was *pure gold,* just like the seed it had sprung from.

The Angel appeared again. He kissed the rose, then said "This rose will soon bring you hope for love and joy." Then, he departed.

Nicola was truly amazed at what she had seen. Her broken heart began to heal, filled with new-found hope.

The following morning, Nicola returned to the center of the forest. She was so delighted to see that the roses were starting to bloom. Each rose was bright red, except for the one in the center. It was pure gold, as if it had been created by the finest goldsmith in the kingdom. It appeared to be worthy of a princess to wear on a chain around her neck, or even a queen. Nicola reached out, and touched it lightly. Its petals were soft, as any other rose. "This is truly a mystery to me…" She murmured to herself, "How can this be possible?"

"All things are possible," a familiar voice said, "to those who have faith." Startled, Nicola jumped back. Then, she looked up to see the Angel standing there, smiling at her. Then, he kissed the rose and then said "This rose will lead you to a life filled with happiness, and love." Then, he flew away.

His words filled her heart with hope.

Every day, Nicola returned to the center of the forest, to sit by her rosebush. She found much peace there, meditating and praying. She thanked God for the rose, and the hope and joy that it filled her heart with each day.

Then, one day she returned to the rosebush only to find that the golden rose was gone! Somebody had just plucked it, and taken it away. Nicola began to cry, and her hope was fading…for the Angel had told her that the rose would lead her to happiness and love. "Surely now, my hope of finding happiness is gone," She wept.

Again, the Angel appeared to her. "Hold onto your faith." He said, "On the other side of the forest is a long path, that leads to a small kingdom called Zalian. Go there, and ask the king if he has seen your golden rose."

Nicola dried her tears, and nodded. She had faith that the Angel's words were true, and faith that she'd find her rose again. She quickly headed through the forest, and down the long path to Zalian…

~ ~ ~

Meanwhile, a lonesome prince sits by a window inside a large marble castle. In his hand is a rose made of pure gold. He asked himself, "How could it be possible to grow such a flower in the middle of the forest?"

Nicola had finally reached the gate to the kingdom of Zalian. She was not only tired but rather intimidated about meeting the King. She knew not what to say to him, but had Faith that God would put the words into her heart at the right time. An angel of the lord had led her to this place…and surely he would not mislead her.

She passed through the gate, took a deep breath, and bravely headed toward the castle. Then, Nicola knocked on its huge oak door. As it opened, the palace guard seemed surprised to see this meek, soft-spoken peasant girl standing in front of him. "I'm here to see the King," she said.

"King Thomas?" The guard said, "What do you want to see him about?"

"My golden rose," Nicola said. "The rose I planted in the deepest part of the forest."

"My dear," the guard said as he shook his head. "Go home, and plant another rose just like the one you've lost. For since the king's son refuses to part with the one he found today, King Thomas has declared that anyone who comes to claim it." He cleared his throat. "Shall be declared a thief, and thrown in the dungeon."

Nicola gasped, and shuddered at the thought. "But it's *my rose!*" She said, certainly the king and his son would understand…"

"Poor girl," The Guard said, "You do not know King Thomas. He is reluctant to believe anything without irrefutable proof."

Nicola sighed, as the guard closed the door. *Irrefutable proof…*she thought to herself, *well I still have the silver seed.*

She realized God would not have led her there if any harm would come to her. So relying on faith, she knocked on the door again.

"What do you want now, foolish girl?" The guard said, "I told you that the King would never believe your story, nor will he let you have your rose—"

"Please, can I at least see the rose again?" Nicola pleaded.

"Well, um…"

"That's all I ask. Just let me see it again. Let me see that it is well taken care of, and has not wilted." she said, managing a half-smile. "Then I'll be gone. I promise." The guard nodded, "wait here." He said, "I shall ask the King."

Nicola waited patiently after a few minutes…and then, the guard returned. "Sorry, dear child." He said, "King Thomas will not let you enter without undeniable proof that the rose was yours."

"Not even to catch just a glimpse of it?" Nicola begged, "Just to see that it is all right, and in good hands?"

"The King suspects that you would sneak in, and attempt to steal it."

Nicola thought for a moment; then she said "I have undeniable proof that the rose is mine. I have another seed in my pocket. May I show it to the King?"

"Wait one minute," The guard said again. He went back inside, and closed the door. Nicola relied on pure faith…she had no proof that the silver seed would grow another rose, just like the first one. It may grow just a silver rose, but she hoped would be proof enough. She also thought it may not grow anything at all…but she had to take a chance.

The guard opened the door, "Okay dear." He said, "You may come in. You may show the seed to the King."

He held the door opened for her as she walked in. The peasant girl, entering the castle for the first time, felt a strange sense of bravery and confidence. She entered the throne room where the King sat stoical. He looked upon her with an expression of skepticism, and doubt. "Your majesty," the Guard said. "This is Nicola, the young girl who came seeking the rose."

"HER?" The king said, "Bah! Look at that tattered dress. She is a mere peasant. How could she possibly afford a rose made of pure gold?"

"Begging your pardon, your highness," She said. "I did not buy the rose with money. I grew it in the forest out of a tiny golden seed."

"RUBBISH!" The king said, "Such things are impossible."

"But, it's true!" Nicola said, "Just look." She reached into the pocket of her skirt, and pulled out the little satchel. She placed the seed into her hand, and held it out for the King to see. "See. It grew from a seed just like this, only golden. This is the second seed the Minister gave me."

"Hmm." The king said as he eyed it skeptically. "You must be the daughter of some silversmith, who could make such things for you…so that you can go around and play these games. And, fool us into believing that you can grow roses made of gold.

"Guards," He said, "I've heard enough of this! Take her to the dungeon." Two more guards came in and grabbed Nicola's arms. As they tried to drag her out of the throne room, she shouted, "But I have proof!" She continually protested, "I can show you. Let me prove it."

At that moment, the King's son ran downstairs. "Father, what is this ruckus?" He had in his hand Nicola's rose. "Who's that girl?" He said, stopping dead in his tracks. Prince Scion smiled at her.

"The Rose," Nicola said, as she saw him. "My Golden Rose." She smiled, glad to see that it was indeed in good hands. The hands of a handsome prince.

"Father, let the girl go." He said, "She has clearly committed no crime here."

"Hmph!" The King said, "she came here with some crazy story about planting the rose, in efforts to steal it from you!"

"I did not lie!" She protested. "And, you may ask the guard at the gate if you don't believe me. I only asked that I could see the rose, to make sure that it was okay. I see that it's fine now and that it has not wilted. The Prince is worthy of the rose, let him keep it. I'll go now."

"How do we know that by setting you free, you're not going to use the seed to trick anyone else?" King Thomas said.

"I have no need to trick anyone," Nicola said. "I just want to go and plant it, and grow another rose. Let me go. Please." She pleaded.

"Absolutely not!"

"Father!" Prince Scion ordered, "Release her! This is ridiculous!"

Nicola struggled to get free, from the guards. Prince Scion tried to pull one of the men away that had a firm grip on her right arm, and as he did so the seed slipped from her hand. Realizing this, Nicola burst out "Oh my gosh! Where did it go?!"

It had fallen right on a crevice between the flagstone tiles of the floor. King Thomas got up from his throne and set his foot right on top of it. Then he ground it into the floor with his boot, crushing it and pushing it down into the crevice.

"There!" He said, "Now no more of this nonsense. As you wish son. Guards, let her go."

Nicola fell to her knees, trying to peer down into the crack in the floor. It was absolutely irretrievable. She began to cry, her tears falling onto the floor. The kind prince helped her up. "It's gone!" Nicola cried, "gone."

Suddenly, voices could be heard. "What was that?" The Prince said.

"I hear singing!" One of the palace guards exclaimed. "Beautiful singing!"

"Silence." The king ordered, "Stop that music!"

The ground rumbled slightly. The music grew louder, and the throne room was filled with an ethereal light. Out of the crevice between the flagstones shot a tiny plant. A rosebush had just started to sprout. "What? NO!" The king said, leaning forward for a closer look. "That is not possible!"

Suddenly the throne room was filled with angels, singing the most beautiful sweet sound. Nicola dried her tears, and smiled. The Rosebush grew up from the floor; even larger than the first.

Soon, the angels surrounded it. They kissed every tiny bud. Nicola smiled, as hope again filled her heart. She knew what would happen next.

Indeed, gold and silver roses came into full bloom all over the bush.

The solemn old King's eyes grew large. Then, the corners of his mouth started to turn up. "HA!" He exclaimed, "Lovely! Just lovely! But how can this be?"

"Miracles happen every day, King Thomas." An angel said to him. "You just have to open your heart, and believe."

A few months later, the King was pleased to hold a grand royal wedding in the Throne Room, which by now had become famous for its rosebush of gold and silver that grew right up from the floor.

The roses remained in full bloom, for the wedding of Prince Scion and his beautiful bride Nicola. And the angels sang them a lovely chorus as they became man and wife.

And, of course…
They lived happily ever after in the spirit of Faith, Hope and Love.

Hans Christian Andersen's

The Red Shoes

ONCE upon a time there was little girl named Karen, who was pretty and dainty. In summer time she was obliged to go barefoot because she was poor; and in winter she had to wear large wooden shoes which made her little instep grow quite red.

In the middle of the village lived an old shoemaker's wife; she sat down and made, as well as she could, a pair of little shoes out of some old pieces of red cloth. They were clumsy, but she meant well, for they were intended for the little Karen.

She received the shoes and wore them for the first time on the day of her mother's funeral. They were certainly not suitable for mourning; but Karen had no others, and so she put her bare feet into them and walked behind the humble coffin.

Just then a large old carriage came by, and in it sat an old lady; she looked at the little girl, and taking pity on her, said to the clergyman, "Look here, if you will give me the little girl, I will take care of her."

Karen believed that this was all on account of the red shoes, but the old lady thought them hideous, and so they were burnt. Karen herself was dressed very neatly and cleanly; she was taught to read and to sew, and people said that she was pretty. But the mirror told her, "You are more than pretty—you are beautiful."

One day the Queen was traveling through that part of the country, and had her little daughter, the Princess with her. All the people, including Karen, streamed towards the castle, where the little Princess, in fine white clothes, stood before the window and allowed herself to be stared at. She wore neither a train nor a golden crown, but beautiful red morocco shoes; they were indeed much finer than those which the shoemaker's wife had sewn for little Karen. There is really nothing in the world that can be compared to red shoes!

Karen was now old enough to be confirmed in the Church; she received some new clothes, and she was also to have some new shoes. The rich shoemaker in the town took the measure of her little foot in his own room, in which there stood great glass cases full of pretty shoes and white slippers. It all looked very lovely, but the old lady could not see very well, and therefore did not get much pleasure out of it. Amongst the shoes stood a pair of red ones, like those which the princess had worn. How beautiful they were! The shoemaker said that they had been made for a count's daughter, but that they had not fitted her.

"I suppose they are of shiny leather?" asked the old lady. "They shine so."

"Yes, they do shine," said Karen. They fitted her, and were bought. But the old lady knew nothing of their being red, for she would never have allowed Karen to be confirmed in red shoes, as she was now to be.

Everybody looked at her feet, and the whole of the way from the church door to the choir it seemed to her as if even the ancient figures on the monuments, in their stiff collars and long black robes, had their eyes fixed on her red shoes. It was only of these that she thought when the clergyman laid his hand upon her head and spoke of the holy baptism, of the covenant with God, and told her that she was now to be a grown-up Christian. The organ pealed forth solemnly, and the sweet children's voices mingled with that of their old leader; but Karen thought only of her red shoes. In the afternoon the old lady heard from everybody that Karen had worn red shoes. She said that it was a shocking thing to do, that it was very improper, and that Karen was always to go to church in future in black shoes, even if they were old.

On the following Sunday there was Communion. Karen looked first at the black shoes, then at the red ones—looked at the red ones again, and put them on. The sun was shining gloriously, so Karen and the old lady went along the footpath through the corn, where it was rather dusty. At the church door stood an old crippled soldier leaning on a crutch; he had a wonderfully long beard, more red than white, and he bowed down to the ground and asked the old lady whether he might wipe her shoes. Then Karen put out her little foot too. "Dear me, what pretty dancing-shoes!" said the soldier. "Sit fast, when you dance," said he, addressing the shoes, and slapping the soles with his hand. The old lady gave the soldier some money and then went with Karen into the church.

All the people inside looked at Karen's red shoes, and all the figures gazed at them; when Karen knelt before the altar and put the golden goblet to her mouth, she thought only of the red shoes. It seemed to her as though they were swimming about in the goblet, and she forgot to sing the psalm, forgot to say the "Lord's Prayer."

Now every one came out of church, and the old lady stepped into her carriage. But just as Karen was lifting up her foot to get in too, the old soldier said: "Dear me, what pretty dancing shoes!" and Karen could not help it, she was obliged to dance a few steps; and when she had once begun, her legs continued to dance. It seemed as if the shoes had got power over them. She danced round the church corner, for she could not stop; the coachman had to run after her and seize her. He lifted her into the carriage, but her feet continued to dance, so that she kicked the good old lady violently. At last they took off her shoes, and her legs were at rest.

At home the shoes were put into the cupboard, but Karen could not help looking at them.

Alas, the old lady fell ill, and it was said that she would not rise from her bed again. She had to be nursed and waited upon, and this was no one's duty more than Karen's. But there was a grand ball in the town, and Karen was invited. She looked at the red shoes, saying to herself that there was no sin in doing that. She put the red shoes on, thinking there was no harm in that either. So she went to the ball and commenced to dance.

However, when she wanted to go to the right, the shoes danced to the left, and when she wanted to dance up the room, the shoes danced down the room, down the stairs through the street, and out through the gates of the town. She danced, and was obliged to dance, far out into the dark wood. Suddenly something shone up among the trees, and she believed it was the moon, for it was a face. But it was the old soldier with the red beard; he sat there nodding his head and said: "Dear me, what pretty dancing shoes!"

She was frightened, and wanted to throw the red shoes away; but they stuck fast. She tore off her stockings, but the shoes had grown fast to her feet. She danced and was obliged to go on dancing over field and meadow, in rain and sunshine, by night and by day—but by night it was most horrible.

Karen danced out into the open churchyard; but the dead there did not dance. They had something better to do than that. She wanted to sit down on the pauper's grave where the bitter fern grows; but for her there was neither peace nor rest. And as she danced past the open church door she saw an angel there in long white robes, with wings reaching from his shoulders down to the earth; his face was stern and grave, and in his hand he held a broad shining sword.

"Dance you shall," said he. "Dance in your red shoes till you are pale and cold, till your skin shrivels up and you are a skeleton! Dance you shall, from door to door, and where proud and wicked children live you shall knock, so that they may hear you and fear you! Dance you shall, dance—!"

"Mercy!" cried Karen. But she did not hear what the angel answered, for the shoes carried her through the gate into the fields, along highways and byways, and unceasingly she had to dance.

One morning she danced past a door that she knew well; they were singing a psalm inside, and a coffin was being carried out covered with flowers. Then she knew that she was forsaken by every one and castigated by the angel of God.

She danced, and was obliged to go on dancing through the dark night. The shoes bore her away over thorns and stumps till she was all torn and bleeding; she danced away over the heath to a lonely little house. Here, she knew, lived the executioner; and she tapped with her finger at the window and said, "Come out, come out! I cannot come in, for I must dance."

The executioner said: "I don't suppose you know who I am. I strike off the heads of the wicked, and I notice that my axe is tingling to do so."

"Don't cut off my head!" said Karen, "for then I could not repent of my sin. But cut off my feet with the red shoes."

And then she confessed all her sin. And, the executioner struck off her feet with the red shoes. Then, the shoes danced away with the little feet across the field into the deep forest.

So in pity, he carved her a pair of wooden feet and some crutches, and taught her a psalm which is always sung by sinners. She kissed the hand that guided the axe, and went away over the heath.

"Now, I have suffered enough for the red shoes," Karen said. "I will go to church, so that people can see me." And she went quickly up to the church-door; but when she came there, the red shoes were dancing before her, and she was frightened, and turned back.

During the whole week she was sad and wept many bitter tears, but when Sunday came again she said, "Now I have suffered and striven enough. I believe I am quite as good as many of those who sit in church and give themselves airs." And so she went boldly on; but she had not got farther than the churchyard gate when she saw the red shoes dancing along before her. Then she became terrified, and turned back and repented right heartily of her sin.

Then, Karen went to the parsonage, and begged that she might be taken into service there. She said that she would be industrious, and do everything that she could; she did not mind about the wages as long as she had a roof over her, and was with good people. The pastor's wife had pity on her, and took her into service. And she was industrious and thoughtful. She sat quiet and listened when the pastor read aloud from the Bible in the evening. All the children liked her very much, but when they spoke about dress and grandeur and beauty she would shake her head.

On the following Sunday they all went to church, and she was asked whether she wished to go too; but, with tears in her eyes, she looked sadly at her crutches. And then the others went to hear God's Word, but she went alone into her little room; this was only large enough to hold the bed and a chair. Here she sat down with her hymn-book, and as she was reading it with a pious mind, the wind carried the notes of the organ over to her from the church, and in tears she lifted up her face and said: "O God! help me!"

Suddenly, the sun shone so brightly, and right before her stood an angel of God in white robes; it was the same one whom she had seen that night at the church-door. He no longer carried the sharp sword, but a beautiful green branch, full of roses; with this he touched the ceiling, which rose up very high, and where he had touched it there shone a golden star. He touched the walls, which opened wide apart, and she saw the organ which was pealing forth. Karen saw the pictures of the old pastors and their wives, and the congregation sitting in the polished chairs and singing from their hymn-books. The church itself had come to the poor girl in her narrow room, or the room had gone to the church. She sat in the pew with the rest of the pastor's household, and when they had finished the hymn and looked up, they nodded and said, "It was right of you to come, Karen."

"It was mercy," said she.

The organ played and the children's voices in the choir sounded soft and lovely. The bright warm sunshine streamed through the window into the pew where Karen sat, and her heart became so filled with it, so filled with peace and joy, that it broke. Her soul flew on the sunbeams to Heaven. And no one there ever asked about the *Red Shoes.*

I have always considered it a strange, yet amazing coincidence that the heroine of this story is named Karen—as that is my name. The story is very much like my own testimony of Salvation. How my unhealthy obsession with ballet, and becoming the perfect ballerina led to an eating disorder. It was sacrificing what I wanted for what God wanted, and crying out to God for mercy and salvation—let a lone a prayer for healing—that changed me in an instant.

This story has always been quite special to me, and that's why I chose to include it in this issue.

WORD SEARCH ANSWER KEY:

```
   A B C D E F G H I J K L M
 1 R I N G S A R M O R E G A
 2 J E H C A S T L E K I N G
 3 O T O L E M A C H W K S R
 4 U D B K S A N P S N N P D
 5 R R B S N I N E I O R E N
 6 N A I D R A U G G I P A N
 7 E Z T P O P H A E N I R P
 8 Y I S L C T R S O L H S M
 9 S W S U I D T I Y S S O O
10 F W W I N V T T N I D O D
11 S E O I U A E Z I C N T S
12 I R L R V I M T H L E H I
13 I E L L D R O O A L I S W
14 D R A G O N R I D E R A S
15 S S H E A W C A L E F Y T
16 R E Y C G O S D S E E E S
17 E U L M W D M H J V A R D
18 L O H P B A E V I C C E F
19 V I T T I O I L H P S A L
20 E Y A D R C L I W S O W A
21 S T E R T A N S H O A E T
22 Q N D O G G G I S R N R T
23 U R R E S Y E N R O I K R
24 E Y R O D L L I I P R O U
25 S S O O D S O O P K E C S
26 T W S H P R O P H E T S T
```

(E11, N) Unicorns
(C2, S) Hobbits
(L25, NW) Cross
(A9, SE) Sword
(J20, SW) Shield
(A17, S) Elves
(F4, SE) Angels
(B9, N) Wizard
(E26, E) Prophet

(L4, SW) Priest
(D7, NE) Prince
(L20, SW) Warrior
(K15, N) friendship
(A10, SE) fellowship
(M22, S) trust
(A22, S) quest
(A2, S) journey
(D2, E) castle
(J24, NW) principles
(M15, SW) teachings
(B15, SE) symbols
(C22, N) Deathly Hallows
(A1, E) Rings
(M17, NW) Defeat Evil
(H18, SW) Victory
(J2, E) King
(M13, N) Wisdom
(J17, SW) villagers
(M18, NW) freedom
(F7,

SE) princess
(M11, SW) shieldmaiden
(H6, W) guardian
(L23, NW) knowledge
(K3, SW) Knight
(J25, NW) King Arthur
(H3, W) Camelot
(I26, NW) Holy Grail
(F9, NE) Dragons
(A14, E) Dragonrider
(L8, S) Sooth Sayer
(L3, S) Spear
(F1, E) armor
(B15, NE) salvation
(A19, NE) volcano
(E13, NE) diety
(C8, SE) Sun

41

Feel free to cut out this page and mail in to subscribe.

FULL ARMOR MAGAZINE

SUBSCRIBE NOW!

___ 8 issues, $20.99

___ 4 issues, $15.99

Payment method:
__Check
__Money order
__Paypal Invoice (please provide email address)

Mailing address:_____
_____
_____

Special instructions:_____

Please mail to:
Dragondreamz Publications
c/o K. Crumley
430 Bechman Street
Springdale, PA 15144

Please allow 4-5 business days for delivery.

www.ingramcontent.com/pod-product-compliance
Lightning Source LLC
Chambersburg PA
CBHW041555120626
46551CB00002B/219